DOG'S
COLOURFUL DAY

Canadian edition produced for
Prospero Books
a division of Chapters Inc.

Devised and produced by
Tucker Slingsby Ltd
Berkeley House,
73 Upper Richmond Road
London SW15 2SZ

Text and illustrations © 2000 Tucker Slingsby Ltd

All rights reserved. No part of this publication may be reproduced or transmitted in any form or by any means,
electronic or mechanical, including photocopying, recording, or any information storage and retrieval system,
without permission in writing from the copyright holders.

Designed by Helen James

ISBN 1-55267-048-1
Printed and bound in Singapore

1 3 5 7 9 10 8 6 4 2

Dog's
COLOURFUL DAY

A Messy Story about Colours and Counting

Emma Dodd

PROSPERO
B·O·O·K·S
A DIVISION OF CHAPTERS INC.

Once upon a time
there was a dog
called Dog.

He was white with
one black spot
on his left ear.

At breakfast time
Dog sat under
the table.

Splat!
A dollop of
red jam landed
on his back.

Now Dog had two spots.

After breakfast, Dog went to the park.

He ran past the man
painting the front door.

Splish!
His tail dipped
into the blue paint.

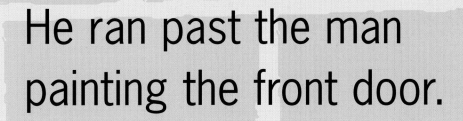

Now Dog had three spots.

In the park, Dog
rolled on the grass.

Squash! The grass left a green stain

on his white coat .

Now Dog had
four spots.

Dog saw a little boy
eating chocolate.
Scrummy!

The boy gave Dog
a chocolatey pat.

Now Dog had
five spots.

A bee buzzed
up to see what
was going on.

Swish! The bee dropped yellow pollen dust as it flew by.

Now Dog had six spots.

Dog trotted on through the park.

Splosh!
A drop of pink ice-cream landed on his right ear.

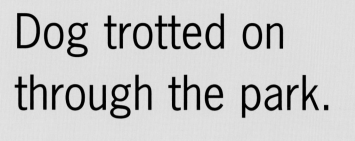

Now Dog had
seven spots.

Time to go home.

A ball bounced in a puddle.

Splash!

A blob of grey mud
stuck to Dog.

Now Dog had eight spots.

In front of the gate, Dog trod on a carton of orange juice.

Squish!
A patch of orange appeared on his leg.

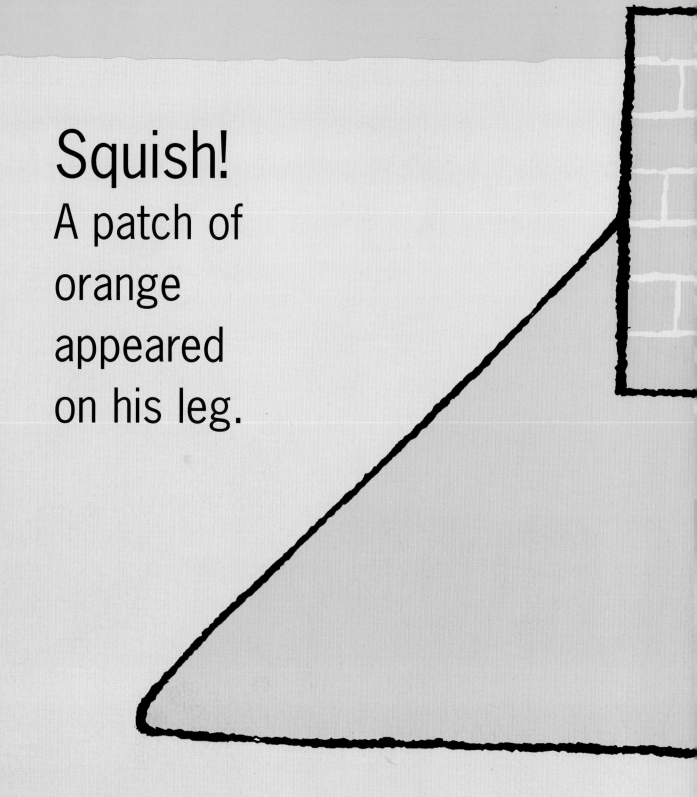

Now Dog had nine spots.

Dog arrived home. He ran to play with Vicky.

Splodge!
Purple ink from Vicky's felt pen went on Dog's head.

Now Dog had ten spots.

Vicky looked down at Dog.
She counted his colourful spots.

1   2   3   4   5

6 7 8 9 10!

Vicky looked more closely.
Dog had...

a red
spot of
jam,

a blue
blob of
paint,

a green
stain of
grass,

a yellow
patch of
pollen,

a brown
smear of
chocolate,

a pink
drop of
ice-cream,

a grey splodge
of mud,

an
orange
splash of
juice

and,
of course,
a black spot
on his left ear!

a purple
ink
mark,

'You need
a bath,
Dog!'

When Dog went to bed he had one black spot on his left ear.

What a colourful day, Dog!